The Search for Internal Universality

Becoming Divine.

Rashad Hedgepeth

Dedicated to:

Every soul that lay eyes upon these words.

There exists an infinite amount of potential stored deep, within each one of us.

We must shift our thinking so that the sky is no longer seen as a limit. Ultimately, we are limitless...

To the cosmos and beyond.

Table of Content

Lost Soul: Looking for a Way

MAN OF STEEL

I told myself today would be the day to take it easy.
But it seems as if the people need me.
However, assuming can be deceiving and these days,
finding drugs are a little too easy.
Sadly, it's the only thing that's relieving-
out of mind but still breathing.
Staying on track isn't so easy.
So, I'm leaving.
Could it be?
Lost my ways and found nothing?
Always down, but up to something.
Music bumping, steady jumping, always constant.
Never nonsense, always honest.
Somewhat careless, should be cautious.
Feeling nauseous, mind is toxic.
Shall I toss it in the closet?
Stop it!
This knowledge will be acknowledged.
I'm aware and conscious, being a light amongst the zombies.
Really not belonging.
But life is pain, and we numb it.
Assuming that's the only assumption.
A dysfunction at the function.
Faded off man-made substance
as if life is redundant.
You can't tell us nothing.
Just souls in need of loving.
But we go out and judge them.
And I'm speaking from experience.
I was once slight delirious.
Doing things, I never did.
Just a kid trying to live.
Lots to do, tons to feel.
It's getting hot, I want chill.
Get to going, like a wheel.
Just a man, made of steel.
Kryptonite made me ill.

But surviving kept me real.
Now I think I know the deal.
It wasn't sealed.
Second life...I wasn't killed.

RIGID ROADS

When the road gets rigid...
I pay my notebook a visit...
I've been visiting quite often.
Suppressed, & depressed but I write softly.
Now it's 8am, where's my coffee?
White chocolate latte!
Maybe a few blunts to ease my body.
Now the waters I tread don't seem so rocky.
But still cold and shocking!
Swallowing me whole like a bad hobby.
I'll give myself freely, no need to rob me.
I'm on my way to the top.
Please   don't   stop   me!

HOLLOW ME

Look at me.
Just a hollow me.
Can't you see that something is bothering me?
Everywhere I go these monsters are following.
Every day is Halloween.
Constantly fondling my fears irresponsibly.
Stealing my sovereignty like armed robbery.
They've done wrongly.
Haunting me in this peculiar anomaly.
Hey! I'm just a man with many faces,
stuck in place being complacent.
Thoughts away from being crazy.
But it's okay with me.
I took interest, and now we're dating.
But there's still a hole inside of me that's vacant.
Been that way for a while.
I think I need a vacation
and a few days of meditating.
So, I can throw away this picture I been painting,
I believe it must be tainted.
From day-to-day basics
becoming sour.
I can taste it.
Spent too much time getting faded.
Luckily it didn't go wasted, and I didn't go crazy.
Odd enough to say, I guess it made me
stop chasing the fast pace of life I was chasing.
It was dangerous and became abrasive.
I was too scared to face it.
So, I created this mental basement,
where my thoughts roam around racing.
Trying to escape from my mind
to the space between the lines on this page.
Creepy feeling taking over now,
I think I need some sage.
Before I change my ways.
Bottom out & become a renegade.

And stay that way...
till I'm old aged.

PEACE OF MIND

I've been searching for a peace of mind
but can't seem to find it.
Things were better back then.
But time can't be rewound.
I can't even fix my lips to begin to lie.
I've had a tough week.
A task, nonetheless,
to decode the things. I wrote and need to read.
Bad taste in my mouth, like I ingested bleach.
Within the clouds lies my sanity.
But it's out of reach.
Running low on sleep.
No desire to eat.
Just to exist and be.
While my heart's wrapped in thorns starting to bleed,
smoke is filling my lungs and I need to breathe.
I should've known better.
I'm just a clever fella with a trick up his sleeve
but I'm heading back to my roots.
Replacing bad habits with something positive.
That's if I choose.
I'm at war with myself and no one is calling a truce.
What am I to do?
All I heard were these few words when all was said and through:
A wise man and a fool have a lot in common.
Which one are you?
Shatter minded I responded, "Both of the two!"
In a bind, I've been trying to get loose.
Detaching from my old self to begin anew.
I looked inside to find these jewels.
I'll give 'em to you, as proof
that   you   can   do   whatever   it   is   that   you   want   to   do!

SMALL TALK

Let's skip the small talk.
That insignificant part.
Let's aim higher.
Converse on your heartfelt desires.
I can't be the only one shooting for the stars.

LOOK:

There's one for each of us.
Ain't that marvelous?
Golden illuminated stardust scattered across the universe.
That's you & I.
Right up there in the sky.
We'll make it if we try.

ADDICTIONS

We all have addictions, and I have one too many to list them.
Or even fix them!
Got sight on my desires but they're off in the distance.
I really hope I haven't missed it.
See, I know my mission.
I was daydreaming and had a vison.
The dimensions went shifting.
But I was too busy being busy to listen
or, even pay attention when life started to mention:
Young man,
you're slipping and acting totally different.
But you can't even admit it.
Because you steady mixing the things you shouldn't mix.
Losing your soul, playing a role within this dirty trick.
When all I was really looking for was a little kick, to keep me going.
Like the words in this poem, how it keeps my life flowing.
I guess a wise man really does learn from a fool's mistakes
and a fool learns from his own.
Traveling down a path of reaping what he has sown.
The good, the bad, and so on.
Until he finds a place where he belongs.
Like the bottom of the bottle.
It'll never leave him alone.
Overthinking his life, feeling a surge in adrenochrome.
Paralyzed, he's falling into a frenzy of agitation.
So, he must close his eyes to use his imagination
to ignore all infatuations and proclaim emancipation
from   the   mental   slavery...he's   endured   lately.

FORGOTTEN

Sometimes, it seems as if people have forgotten about me.
I could never be forgotten.
Either way, stopping isn't an option.
Action packed, no longer watching.
Take caution, trying to rock out, may end you in a mosh pit.
Nose runny like faucets.
Bad habit can't toss it, forget it, I can't drop it.
So, it's here in my pocket,
maybe in my moccasins.
That's obvious.
A little androgynous.
Gave my heart to an audience.
Isn't that marvelous?
Had to make a choice & chose opposite.
Made me more prominent.
Could never become redundant, always useful for something.
Do it like it's nothing.
I popped up so sudden.
Like someone pushed too many buttons...

EZ

It's easy to make a buck.
It's tougher to make a difference.
I must define my hindrance.
It was "all me" from the beginning□.
Now I have a desire to change that before I'm finished.
You see...a mind like mine is usually found in a clinic.
Locked away in a cage somewhere from sinning.
Counting down the minutes.
Now, close your eyes & light some incense.
This life has been intense.
Got me here venting, feeling all this tension.
Broke the pendant I've been clenching.
A non-attendance in my attention landed me right in detention.
Came out with a beautiful invention.
Under the influence, squinting, deep down feeling offended,
short winded, with a lack of interest.
Are we going or are we coming?
I really can't tell the difference.
I just need a bank full of digits.
This hyper fidget misfit will never sit back and kick it.
I'm completely committed.
Putting my feelings on exhibit.
Dedicated and consistent.
Isn't this magnificent?
On a full-blown mission trying to escape a mental prison.
Never allowed visits.
No window shooting star wishes.
Just examining religions & aligning my intentions with illuminated visions.

BRAGGING RIGHTS

What will I do with the time I've been given?
Goal driven.
Feelings get written in a cloud of smoke, getting lifted.
Feeling terrific.
It's been rather splendid.
Blessed with "the life" and I've been living it.
Never do it different.
Speak it clearly so you listen, conscious talk grabbed your attention.
But I'm just seeking redemption from indecent decisions.
Hard to see clear with a distorted vision.
So, I guess I'll follow my intuition.
Plucking coins into a fountain...wishing.
Praying my intentions are efficient.
Or I shall send these words into collision.
Continuously spinning, I'll have 'em asking, "Who is it?"
Nothing more than the Poetic Pisces Wizard,
walk a straight whisker.
Faded off elixir.
Silver tongued trickster.
Verbally painting a picture.
But what's in that mixture?
He's gulping it down by the pitcher.
Sent me off on an adventure
to find my center.
Maybe balance out.
So, I don't get lost in my screams when I shout.
Indulging in all these substances get rid of my doubts.
I wonder what that's all about?
With a back somewhat slouched getting locked in a couch.
But that's when I found my worth & my amount...
Thought things through, then I was out.

(IN)SECURITY

Every time I let someone in,
I'm reminded why I can't secure my insecurities.
Eyes become teary.
Can no longer see clearly.
My EVERYTHING is just blurry.
Depressed and a tight chest, can you cure me?
Clean my soul of the fury.
Lord knows I'm worthy.
Experienced "a lot" quite early.
A clean heart got a little dirty.
Made my mind go swirly.
In the fast lane swerving.
Lot of issues- can't word it.
But on my face- I'll wear it.
And you wonder why I'm lit.
Shoulders sitting ahead getting heavy from the chip.
I could use a lift!
Maybe a ledge to hold onto if I slip.
Peaking off a substance, had my share of sips.
Walking this plank.
Jumping ship.
Moving swift.
Watch me catapult into a triple backflip.
Dive in and take a dip.
Come out prepared and equipped.
Wiser than a pharaoh from Egypt.
I'm not boasting.
These words simply get spoken.
Staying on track, I see my dreams approaching.
Drunk off a magical potion.
Moving in slow motion.
Now we coasting.
Feelings out in the open.
So vulnerable,
I   may   close   them.

STAR SHOOTING

I'm still shooting for the stars!
Just aiming more precisely.
Hoping to approach these obstacles more wisely.
They've become chastising
but I continue rising
above all hate and violence.
My vibrations are too vibrant.
Too outspoken to be silent.
Lost my ways, but somehow found my talent.
Never back down from a challenge!
I've been through the ruins, made a mess from my doings.
In life, I'm a student.
Pioneer of a poetic movement.
Broken.
But still giving my two cents.
Receiving nothing back has become a nuisance.
Got me sinking like cruise-ships.
Influential as Confucius.
But can't find the fuse to my confusions.
The perplexity is no longer amusing.
Muddled in a puddle of losing.
Got me screwed.
But I refuse to stay stuck like glue!
Waters getting choppy now, I could use a canoe.
Maybe a screwdriver to tighten what's loose.
The "bolts" of my mind are what I'm referring to.
Electrical currents of creative juice.
Striking   faster   than   the   Greek   god   Zeus.

FLOW

Life can be scary. In the dark, I'm looking for clarity.
Far from parody, this is poetic soul's charity.
If life was so merrily.
I wouldn't have pack these words like weaponry.
Mixing things, I should have kept separately.
Need a house in the hills of Beverly.
When you carry such a melody.
A sound so heavenly.
Came from life's lessons testing me.
Hallucinations on sesame.
Vices of necessity.
But you'll never get the recipe.
White rabbits & LSD.
A wonderland of ecstasy.
Went deep into the depths of the corners of my mind.
Seek, & ye shall find.
Relaxing on cloud 9.
Stuck between the lines.
Even writing off the page sometimes.

MESSAGE

Let's stand up & speak for what's right.
Instead of out of mind, out of sight.
Like these tears that I wiped, I got issues.
Trashcan full of tissues.
Heart colder than igloos.
I've been misused and abused.
With no other options to choose.
But I stand upright in my shoes, with pain I wish I could soothe.
Looking for the "white" & got stuck with the "blues"
The lines I walk are rather skewed.
Thanks to my alter ego mood.
Spitting lyrical soul food.
A place where I put my foot.
A little soul and spice are all that it took.
Blessed with a tongue that can do no wrong.
I've become fond of where I belong...right there, amid a poem.
What'd ya know, this pen had my back all along.

WHAT TO DO?

What do you do when your words don't carry the weight
they deserve?
Why can't anyone see I have a ton of things to say?
Need someone to relate.
Maybe find an escape
from this cloudy gray day.
Writing away.
Like these rhymes have the solutions to my problems.
Mm...
Either that or a revolver.
Got 1 shot at life.
Why not fly high like a kite?
Or shine bright, like a star in the night!

NOTE TO SELF

On the verge of mental breakdown, lost the ways I thought I found.
This rocky foundation was once so sound.
But this is "me" getting back in bounds.
I'm taking back my sovereignty!
It was never "The Man's" property.
Had me in a daze, thinking unconsciously□ .
Losing my grip, something was bothering me.
Spiritually & psychologically.
Feeling like the anomaly.
Spent too much time pondering.
If this, if that, wondering.
Trying to figure out what's stopping me.
Too afraid to leave it up to chance.
I remember being left in a trance.
Trying to accomplish what I was told I can't.
Infuriation led me here, to this rant.
But this is more like an apology letter to myself.
Written,   sealed,   &   stamped.

GREATNESS

I know why I'm being tested.
Life wants to see how much I'm invested!
Little worries pick away at my mind.
Every nook and cranny they can find.
Greatness is heading my way.
As hard times try to find an escape!
Oh.
All the amazing things to come.
Health, money, and longevity.
A successful recipe, I've been waiting to taste so readily.
Blinded by diamonds and worldly possession.
I feel greatness is headed my direction.
I really need what's owed.
My kingdom, Queen, & gold.
I promise to be courageous and bold.
Stand tall & never fold.
Oh yes!
Greatness is destined for me.
From this very moment on, till as far as the eyes can see.

I'M TIRED

I'm tired.
Tired of not getting what I deserve.
Don't you think after putting in all this hard work
and receiving nothing back hurt?
Tired of being loyal,
when all I get back is deceit.
I been standing on my own two feet.
Tired from getting up from the get down.
When the carpet has been swept from beneath.
Over and over again.
I'm...tired.
I've been feeling this way for way too long.
I asked God to bring more art to my life.
I've already made sacrifices.
I'm tired of zipping my lips to swallow my pride.
Been tired of walking a straight line.
Especially, when I didn't have to walk a line at all.
I'm tired.
Quite tired of being let down.
And for damn sure tired of being left out.
With a frown,
I'm tired.
Where's my piece of the pie?
I'm really tired of waiting.
I'm tired of running thin on patience!
When am I going to get to where I'm supposed to be?
I'm tired of where I been.
I'm sick of being "been"
I'm ready to start living...
And   be!

Finding a Way

WAKE UP

Wake up!
Can't you see so much is corrupt?
Television only told our vision lies.
Behavior modification mastermind in disguise.
Trying to override my intelligence.
Steal my DNA & melanin.
Those in power commit crimes like felons.
Doing things, they will never tell.
But my intuition tells me to pay attention.
The laws changing by the day.
Years go by and I feel more restricted.
A slave to society?
Or slave to a business?
The way they got it scripted, I can no longer see the difference.
Distorting the image.
Putting a blemish on the beautiful picture of living.
But who am I kidding?
Most think I speak gibberish.
They labeled me a sophisticated conspiracist.
But I'm bringing the truth clear like this:
They're really against us.
This is serious.
Or I have I went off the deep-end-delirious?
Ironically, I'm sharing things publicly, I usually speak on secretly.
We steady slaving for a piece of paper distributed unequally!
Tell me why the rich don't give eagerly.
I feel like someone cheated me.
This American Dream deceived me.
Had me thinking I belong.
But all along, racism proved me totally wrong.
From the white house to the black concrete down every
American road
where my ancestors were sold.
So, who are you to tell me that Black isn't really gold?
It's something I know.
WAKE UP!

VIVID

I spend hours in a cubicle.
Sacrificing time for a dollar.
I wished my culture raised me to be frugal.
Instead of carrying a ruger, acting foolish not using my noodle.
Trying to shoot my shot,
though I'm not a shooter.
It took some time to find my inner peace like Buddha.
Feeling better than Kama Sutra.
But still a warrior like Zulu
Skin chocolate like Yoo-hoo.
Favored by God, no Voodoo. □
Growing up now, not thinking how I used to.
I now use my mind, but I'm sure if I lost that.
Things wouldn't be so fine.
So, I thank the powers that be...
I'm in touch with the Divine.
And like the rays from the sun,
I shall shine.

READ MYSELF

Stuck in thought most of the time.
Taking the time to watch & listen to my body...
Shaking, like I drank a pool of coffee Proof, I must treat this
temple more softly.
Remove the toxins that make me foggy.
Trying to keep the morals my Momma taught me.
Everything that glitters isn't gold.
It's just another novelty.
For me to get addicted to and have a problem on my hand that
I'm still solving.
Head spinning faster than a revolving revolver.
I wish I felt calmer.
On this path moving onward.
All alone.
But never a loner.

DO YOU FEEL ME?

Fees here, fees there.
Fees to breathe.
Fees to leave. □
It costs to plant a seed!
Everything is a cost.
Nothing comes cheap.
Beware of anything that's sold free!

BLACK & BROWN

Black & brown skin.
The skin of the earth.
But they treat us like dirt!
Heavily melanated skin isn't a curse.
Rather a blessing given at birth
that can never be reversed.
Socio-economic class inverse.
We last in the race of races.
But should be first!
They destroy the water, air, & land as if it has no worth.
I dream of a Wakanda-like land,
where my people get what they deserve.
The essentials to a happy, thriving life.
Not a life where we continuously
& constantly must put up a fight!

MY 3 W'S

Working, to make a dollar.
Working out, to stay up on my health. □
Writing, to keep my spirit alive.
I been investing in myself.
And not much else.
And that's a whole lot!

CENTERPIECE

People come out nowhere, when you're on your "A" game.
When everything starts to change.
I had to make a name for myself.
Congratulations turn to jealousy. □
But my passion will never become a dread to me.
People should just embrace my art and its fragility.
Instead of trying to capitalize off my ability.
Gaining financial security.
Depending on another, never seemed secure to me.
Pushing my buttons, expecting me to react fiercely.
But I respond so cheerfully, with heartfelt words so dear to me.
I live this life fearlessly.
And I don't mean figuratively.
I asked God to center me
like a centerpiece.

REAL LIFE

Compliance by silence?
No more spiritual, just science.
Numbers & finance.
In the matrix searching for an exit but can't find it.
And all these distractions got me blinded.
Starting to awaken the sleeping giant.
Like the Hulk, I can get violent.
But lately I've been divided.
Stuck in the middle of a mind two sided.
Talk about being indecisive!
Bouncing back and forth between
doing wrong and being righteous.

3/25/20

Feeling out of place.
Heart in a cage.
Empty.
Scatter- brained.
Feeling heated.
Like flames.
Stuck inside out myself.
Pulled the trigger.
But forgot the bullets.
I studied long.
But studied wrong.
Failed the test.
With flying colors.
Made mistakes coherently.
Then cried about them later.
Fighting my ego.
My ego winning.
It's time to throw in the towel.
My   rage   of   guilt.

CHITTER CHATTER

They say life is poetry.
Sometimes a short story.
But a few good choices can add a few more chapters.
A little happiness, & laughter.
Isn't that what we're all after?
Or are we all just evolving backwards?
With a phone, looking for a moment to capture.
As if life was a movie full of actresses & actors.
Being original isn't a factor.
Better off winning a quick cash scratcher.
Just a few thoughts from my brain's chitter chatter.

B2W (BORN TO WIN)

Born to win, wasn't bred to lose.

When hard times got heated, I blew a fuse.

Made it kind of hard for me to obey the rules.

I'd rather stick to my craft like it's made of glue.

Walking this path only traveled by few. □

But can't come to conclude why I spread myself thin, when I know I should recoup□ .

And these issues steady piling on

whenever I try to remove any obstacles that would cause me to lose.

Cut the conversation short with the barrier of bad news.

Been battling my demons.

Been sent through the ringer repeatedly.

But you probably wouldn't believe me, if I told you the things I been through previously.

People backstab and act so deviously.

They play themselves...like a DVD.

MY TRUTH

I have a lot of shameful ways.
Many, that will never be explained.
I just pray that the good I've done doesn't go in vain.
Feeling shameful, guilty, & unworthy.
My emotion made these poems quite lengthy and wordy.
Expressing the issues that concern me.
Like not being enough.
Or am I just ALMOST good enough?
I take this pain and hurt myself further with bad decisions,
followed by action
all these lights & cameras.
But I'm not acting. . .smiling nor laughing.
I'm getting tired of this pattern.
I need a new design.
A little extra strength to free solo this climb up the backside of my
mind.
It spins around in circles like the sand of time.
Now, I'm drunk off the spirit, but not a sip of wine.
I gave it all to God and he gave me a sign.
I'm HIS child.
Even when I act foul, wild, & totally in denial.
Falling short of being a saint.
But this Pisces never sank, I always swim.
All or nothing!
Even when chances looking slim,
don't take it for granted.
I   take   'em...for   the   win.

WHAT IT TAKES TO OVERCOME

I know some people hate me.
But I must continue to show love.
Can't you see I'm free?
No longer shackled by mental chains.
My frame of mind has changed.
Shifted shapes & I'm feeling great.
Today, I'm starting with a new slate.
I took what I had, now look at what I made!
I took lemons and made lemonade.
Now sit back & let me demonstrate.
I'm finished with infatuations, it only put a dent in my savings.
And I always listened to those old folks' saying,
"Work now so you can rest later."
So, I got my eyes on the target like a beam from a laser.
Tunnel visioned, blocking out the naysayer.
I never paid attention to a hater.
Would rather use it as inspiration to become greater.
Remember no one's going to do you any favors.
And handshakes are shaky
so, read the fine print on the papers when you're doing something
major.
And keep up on your health.
Stay sharp as a razor.
And NEVER forget the ways your mama raised ya.

WAKE UP PT. 2

Are we waking up
or just simply trying to adjust?
Fighting amongst one another like we never heard of love.
What if...the enemy wasn't who we thought it was?
We judge one another just because of social stigma.
We all bleed red blood.
That should be enough for us to lift one another up
out the rut
and get out of our own way, if we're stuck.
But I know some people will never change..
Until they experience an unconditional love that can heal all pain.

GROW

Frustrated days spent slaving away.
Working a 9 to 5 at minimum wage.
Just seconds away from bursting into rage.
I must be quick and find a way to change my ways.
The powers that be been mining deep in my mind.
Psychologically trying to find a way to block out my shine.
But I found a way to maneuver.
No more GMO's & sugar.
A.K.A manure.
Not just a smooth talker, I've proved that I'm a doer.
Chakras aligning, heart rising out the sewer.
Innocent like a newborn.
My cold ways turned lukewarm.
Feeling golden, with a charm.
I rose to the occasion when my body rang the alarm.
I was in a deep sleep.
Ingesting this, ingesting that.
Could've ended 6 feet.
But that wasn't meant for me.
Now I overstand, mind over matter.
Because most things...don't really matter.
We're too busy moving forward backwards.
Waiting for something to happen, then reacting afterwards.
Eating fast food.
Getting fatter.
And obesity stabs the heart like a dagger.
Did you know:
Your soul is up for collateral?

SURFACE LEVEL

Most I know, vibrate low
but think they're almighty with a nice car.
Obsessed with the physical and don't know God.
I took time out to get to know Rashad,
since the Most High dwells within.
I'm putting my best foot forward to live this life free of sin.
Figured I'd find the gold within.
Been looking for more than worldly wishes, and all paper printed Benjamins.
Only fruits and veggies go in this engine.
So, when it's all said and done, my 21 grams will take flight into ascension.
Transcending dimensions.
I let go of tension and instilled my intentions.
Traveling a path of Divine intervention.
No longer searching for what's missing.
I read the writing on the wall even when hidden & encrypted.
There's a peaceful sound in silence.
I can tell you; I've listened.
Dissolving desires for diamonds & gold take control, when the soul glistens.
Now I love myself unconditionally.
I'm treating others no differently.

How to Glow 101

No filters, no edits.
The goal is perfection.
Tried to get in where I thought I'd fit in.
Never was accepted.
So, I tuned into myself & detached from deception. Swiftly
changing directions.
Re-engineered...by a divine connection.

WTDB

Writing, thinking, & deep breathing
are the only things that keep me even
when odd feelings creep in.
Seeing *IS* believing, and all my experience made me well-seasoned.
No one said life would be cream and peachy.
Having the odds stacked against me gave me a reason
to stay reaching and overachieving my previous achievements.
I'm just going with the flow now, like I'm One with the breeze.
Remember, only heavy hearts freeze.
It's time to clear the debris.
The heart should be lighter than a feather:
Pure & clean.

MASK

Don't forget your mask.
Be sure to hide your smile.
It isn't as if you've shown it in a while.
So, don't forget your mask.
And remember to have little, to no contact.
Physically, mentally, or even spiritually.
Got me wondering curiously,
is this some sort of tyranny?
The law now says we must wear a mask.
You know...
A good thing never last.
The natural way of life is being attacked.
But, no big deal.
We already disguise personality.
Might as well mask your individuality.
Become a fatality.
Just another socio-economic casualty.
As we get further from ourselves, questioning reality.
I repeat, don't forget your mask.
You'll need it everywhere.
And sure, Black Lives Matter
but they really don't care!
Acting unaware, they're far more concerned with a fair market share.
So, beware.
All incorporated governments follow suit.
We've been told what to do.
But told by whom?
Only the darkest of forces, I assume.
Not to sound like a loose screw, but I wish I knew:
Who controls the fate of me and you?
Somethings are best left for God.
We are living in a time we can't describe.
Racism and COVID taking over our lives.
It's up to you to decipher the difference between the truth and a lie.
They want us standing 6 feet,

until we 6 deep,
with a muzzle over our mouths.
Discouraging us to speak.

INTENTIONS

I intend. . .
I intend to no longer play pretend.
As if everything is okay on my end.
I'd much rather intend.
Intend to ascend. . .
Stop searching for answers and look within.
With intentions to win!
I intend. . .
To face all my fears that I've been swimming in for years.
So, let's make a toast to a great life.
Here.
Cheers!
I intend. . .
To find real love.
Maybe she can mend a broken heart.
Even from a tiny million little pieces.
Fragile things tend to break a lot.
I intend. . .
To bring back all good karma owed
and paint this path I travel gold.
I'll be the light shining bright!
When it's dark & cold.
I do intend. . .
To take my self-centered sins away, becoming my true authentic
self.
No longer disturbing my inner peace
with any substance not meant for me.
I intend. . .
To stay true
and grounded in my roots.
But you know, this cold world trying to shake me loose.
Wanting me to uproot.
But my intentions. . .stuck like glue.

Stumbling upon Self-Realization

SOUL 2 SOUL

I'm not exactly where I want to be.
But I'm a lot better than I used to be.
Had to let things go in order to grow.
Demons of addiction had me in a tight hold.
Chasing after riches.
I thought I was woke.
But a clock is right twice a day.
Even when it's broke.
So, I deeply desire to be authentic.
All the world's fiat money presented, isn't that convincing
for me to go against my mission.

I shall find the gold within my soul before I'm finished.
I'm aligned with a divine lineage.
Didn't apply for a membership.
and the truth can't be told with censored lips.
So, speak wisely when formulating a sentence.
Because the universe is always watching and listening.

SENTIENT

I'm a child of the cosmos.
My heart leads and I follow.
I learned to become whole when I was hollow.
A solid foundation won't topple.
Experienced & knowledgeable.
I'm my own role model.
Depression used to have me feeling like water in a pothole.
But my soul is full of gold like I hit the lotto!

REALITY

Most things are a distraction.
Got you worried about "what" and "when" it happened.
Broadcasted attention, grabbing powerful magic!
When all you really need is detachment.
No need to wait till things get tragic.
Keep in mind, some changes are everlasting
and I wasn't put here to be passive.
My heart is too massive. . .
So, take it from me and put it into action.
I suggest making a change for the better so drastic
that everyone around you will wonder what happened
and you'll be there laughing.
Feeling no sadness.
Floating.
On a wonderful cloud of happiness!

FROM MY SPIRIT

Looking inside myself to get to the root of the issue.
With a wet face, I could use some tissue.
A whole fistful.
Feeling like Mr. pitiful.
Between a rock & a hard place, stuck in the middle.
Realer than any riddle.
Going through hell & expected to be civil
when I'm not feeling well.
Not even a little.
I'm heated with more fire than a kindle.
How did an angel end up in a place so sinful
all the while keeping a smile showing dimples?
It's simple...
One who holds the light must be right...
and gentle.

CHARACTER

If we got paid based on character,
would you be more careful?
Less destructive, and more helpful?
I swear, all this sickness in the world won't let my stomach settle.
So, it's vital I remain mellow when life become too stressful.
And I feel like feeling terrible.
But I'm quick to hide my pain in these parables
when it all become unbearable.
I know I need a miracle.
But I just keep praying, hoping the sick ways of the world are
curable.
Everyone should be balanced.
Mind, body, and spiritual.
Some say it's easier said than done.
Some just say it's difficult.
I'll be self-improving until I reach my pinnacle.
Don't mean to sound cynical.
I decode the symbols like its simple.
Building a pyramid between my mental temples.

MY TRUTH PT. 2

I'm still trying to break bad habits.
Who knew they could be this long-lasting?
In choppy waters, on a kayak paddling.
Stuck in my ways, baffled.
On my high horse & forgot the saddle.
Tuned into myself, got distracted and changed the channel.
Had me lit like the wick of burning candles.
But that's when I found balance.
And the time to discover my talent.
Breaking free from mental confinement,
I was told to meditate my chakras into alignment.
Doing a talking fast, I stay silent. . .
Flowing in the abundance the universe providing.
I'm tired of just "getting by" surviving.
I been self-reflecting, in the deep waters I went diving.
No more going back and forth with myself fighting!
I counted my issues & started dividing.
Executing. . . precisely.

ANGELIC MOTIVATION

I will live.
I will strive.
I *WILL* be. . .more than I ever thought or dreamed I could be.

THE WORDS I LIVE BY

It's best to keep moving forward.
You can miss your chance looking behind.
Those who stay present are the most mindful of the signs.
But can you really see clear, if you're spiritually blind?
I know most of us are just pretending to be fine.
Unaware that we're Divine and truly one of a kind.
Looking for help with no one replying.
Not a soul to confide in.
So, most times, I step off in private.
To gather myself, until the tiny light inside becomes vibrant.
And all my loose ends end up, tied together tightened.
Only positive energy invited.
Embarking on a journey so exciting.
I dropped all anxiety
and chose to be cheerful and lively.
I'm building a life using my psyche.
Never minding those acting shiesty.
I avoid the blade when things get dicey.
With a perspective respected highly.
But I'm still searching for a part of me that's hiding.
Got me on the lookout...eyeing.

LOVE IS MY BELIEF

Every life matters.
But I can show you more than a few of my brothers who've had
their dreams shattered.
Then mislabeled as a hazard until chased down and captured.
I must speak on what's real!
Ain't no programming and propaganda.
This kind of behavior has become standard.
But if racism was a cancer, we'd all have to stand up.
Be the light, and shine by example.
We don't want things to get out of hand
to a point we can't handle.
Sitting empty handed, the building blocks of life seem to be
dismantling.
They want it black vs white.
But don't fall for that scandal.
We are all apart of human nature.
So, tell me...
What's the hate for?
From the rich to the poor,
everyone should pay it forward.
And I'll be doing my part on a poetic forefront.
Now, shift your focus to what's important and try to make better
choices.
Start going with the flow and stop forcing.
Things never go our way when we disregard the problems we've
been avoiding.
But never mind that, we in the fast lane flooring it.
Beautiful settings become distorted and sunny days become
stormy.
Make you quick to change your ways and smell the coffee in the
morning.
I used to think life without a vice was boring.
But then, heart palpitations became alarming.
Now I must live in harmony.
But temptations are forever charming and coming with the force
of an army.
Doing their best to disarm me and harm me.

But I excuse them lightly like, "pardon me."
You are no longer a part of me.

A MOMENT'S PRAYER

Living moment by moment,
Instead of becoming frustrated & explosive.
Many times I be all alone, self-coaching.
Going through things, but staying friendly & approachable.
Leading a life quite notable.
Leaving a light I can show to all.
Chasing my dreams not known to pause or stall.
I'm in this for more than material wishes.
I desire things hardly ever mentioned.
Like wholeness & aura cleansing.
I'm just an old soul with inner wisdom.
Looking for the path to ascension, and a way to detach from the
system.
I want to be a role model for the children.
Rid their mind of negative emotion and anything unfulfilling.
Teach the spoken word of love...and good feelings.

STILL, I RISE (MAYA ANGELOU TRIBUTE)

You may write me down in history.
And tell them I how great I was during my time.
You can cut me out and leave me behind.
But like a thin piece of paper.
I'll rise.

Does my mysteriousness upset you?
Am I supposed to be an average joe and play it cool?
I'd rather back these words up
with a little show and prove.

Just like air & water
that keeps us alive.
Just like an ambitious soul reaching high
still, I'll rise.

Do you want to see me hopeless?
Out on the street homeless?
Head falling like teardrops
from too many horrible moments?

Does my ambition offend you?
Don't you take it awful hard.
The world is just a stage
and I'm simply playing my part.

You may shoot me with your judgments.
You may give me bad energy from your eyes.
You may kill me with your hatefulness.
But still, like my pride, I'll rise.

Does my manliness upset you?
Does it come as a surprise
that I express myself freely?
Can't you tell I'm in love with my mind?

Out of the depths of deep self-reflection.

I rise.
Up from being down, lacking love and affection:
I rise.
I'm the black universe stretching and reaching wide.
The stars are just a fragment of me, burning bright.

Leaving behind nights of terror and fear.
I rise.
Into a vison, I now see myself crystal clear.
I rise.
Bringing the gift my ancestors gave.
These words even help me
find my way.
I rise.
I rise.
I rise.